Judy Moody's

Mini-Mysteries and Other Sneaky Stuff for Super-Sleuths

Megan McDonald
illustrated by Peter H. Reynolds

CANDLEWICK PRESS

Meet Judy Moody, Super-Sleuth

Detective Name: **Judy Drewdy**

(after her all-time favorite
mystery solver, Nancy Drew)

Detective Agency: **Judy Drewdy
Detective Agency**

Toad Pee Tent
117 Croaker Road
Frog Neck Lake, Virginia

Specialties: Finding missing animals,
following suspects,
interviewing witnesses,
code-cracking, cookie-eating

Fellow Agents:

Agent Dills Pickle
(aka Frank)

**Agent Spuds
Houdini**
(aka Rocky)

**Agent James
Madagascar**
(aka Stink)

FILL IN *YOUR* DETECTIVE INFORMATION:

Detective Name:

Detective Agency:

Specialties:

Fellow Agents:

MYODK
(Make Your Own Detective Kit!)

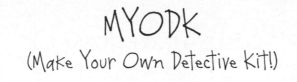

Detective Judy knows that a good detective is ready for anything. You can be prepared for anything, too. MYODK! Make Your Own Detective Kit. Turn the page to see some ideas for must-have items in your kit. Don't leave home without it—you never know what could happen. A real-live mystery could be just a fingerprint away!

COLLECTING EVIDENCE:

- detective notebook (for keeping track of clues, witnesses, and suspects; see p. 10 for tips)
- pencil (for recording information in your notebook)
- zip-top bag (for holding evidence, like pieces of fabric, food wrappers, pet hair, or anything else you might find at the crime scene—Stink's gum wrappers don't count!)
- tweezers (for picking up evidence)

- magnifying glass (for finding fingerprints, footprints, or other hard-to-see evidence—mag-ni-fy-cent!)

DISGUISING YOURSELF:

◎ sunglasses (for changing your appearance
   quickly; also useful on sunny days)

◎ fake noses and mustaches (another
   way to quickly alter your appearance)

◎ eyebrow pencil (for drawing fake mustaches or freckles)

◎ hat and wig (for deep undercover work,
   where not even Jessica Finch will find you!).

Hint: *raid the Halloween costume box.*

SPYING:

◎ binoculars or telescope (for keeping an eye
   on faraway suspects)

◎ mirror (for seeing people or things—or
   Stink!—behind you or for decoding mirror
   writing!)

◎ walkie-talkies (for communicating
   with fellow agents)

OTHER THINGS THAT MIGHT COME IN HANDY:

 ◉ flashlight (for nighttime stakeouts, seeing in dark basements or attics, or hiding in closets)

◉ money (for paying a reward or buying supplies; if you don't have any money, try asking your brother or sister to loan you some)

 ◉ bobby pins (for picking locks—or keeping messy hair out of your eyes!)

◉ small cup (handy for listening through walls)

- SOS lipstick (for writing HELP messages!)

- watch with alarm (in case you doze off on stakeouts)

- snacks (cracking cases makes you hungry)

- gum (what's a gum-shoe without it?)

- brush or tape (for dusting for fingerprints)

- ruler (for measuring footprint sizes)

Make a Detective Notebook

Plumbers in green van

JACK FROST?

JESSICA FINCH (HA,HA — I WISH!)

Old Lady, begins with an S

You'll need:

◈ A spiral-bound notepad that is small enough to fit into a pocket

◈ A small pencil or pen

WHAT TO INCLUDE IN YOUR NOTEBOOK:

Facts about the case

- date and time of the crime
- witnesses and information you gain from interviews with them
- evidence found at the scene of the crime
- a list of possible suspects

Diagrams, drawings, charts, sketches, and graphs

- the shape and layout of a room
- the placement and size of objects in a crime scene
- the location of all possible entrances and exits from a crime scene

Other visual aids

- A suspect sketch (see p. 43)

Notes

Just the facts, Judy! Try to stick to the most important facts you find. Put only one fact on a page. At the top of each page, write the heading in large letters (i.e., DATE AND DAY, TIME, WITNESS BY NAME, etc.) so it's easy to find again later. Below each fact, list important details. As you make notes, try answering a detective's most important questions: who, what, when, where, and why.

Detective's Dictionary

alibi: *an excuse used to prove a person's innocence*
example: Judy's alibi was airtight. There's no way she could have "borrowed" a quarter from Stink since she was at Jessica Finch's house all day.

clue: *something that helps to solve a mystery*
example: Stink's white mustache was a clue in the case of the missing milk.

culprit: *the person responsible for a crime*
example: In the case of the missing tuna fish, Mouse was the clear culprit.

deduce: *to come to a conclusion based on facts*

example: Judy deduced that a rabbit had made a snack out of her snowman's nose based on carrot crumbs nearby and paw prints in the snow.

hunch: *a suspicion or guess*

example: Judy couldn't prove it, but she had a hunch Mr. Todd was going to give a pop quiz.

motive: *a person's reason for doing something*

example: In the case of the missing Magic 8 Ball, Mom's motive for moving it was cleaning up Judy's room before Grandma Lou came to visit.

red herring: *a misleading clue; something that diverts attention from the truth*

example: A strawberry bubble-gum wrapper was a red herring in the mystery of the missing watermelon gum. The wrapper drew attention, but was not related to the mystery.

stakeout: *close watch of a location or suspect to collect information*

example: Stink had a stakeout in his back-yard to collect evidence of Bigfoot.

witness: *a person who sees or hears a crime take place*

example: Judy was a witness in the case of the missing math sheet. She saw Mr. Todd put it in the recycling bin by mistake.

Using your notebook and detective skills, try solving the following mini-mystery.

Wherefore Art Thou, Romeo?

MINI-MYSTERY #1

Everyone on the bus!" Mr. Todd said. Class 3T was going on a field trip to the Z-O-O zoo! Judy couldn't wait to see the animals. Mostly she couldn't wait to see Romeo and Juliet, the new king penguins. Mom had shown her a newspaper article about these new additions to the zoo. They were about to hatch an egg!

The bus pulled up to the zoo just as the front gates were opening. Judy could barely sit still. "Class, we'll start our visit in the bird area," said Mr. Todd. "Follow me."

Bird area? That means penguins! Judy thought.

The students followed Mr. Todd to the bird area, and there, like a frozen wonderland, was the penguin habitat. Judy peered through the tall fence.

"There's Juliet!" she said to Frank. Juliet was balancing an egg on her feet, keeping it warm. And she was making funny chirping sounds.

"Look! The mom and dad penguins take turns keeping the egg warm."

"Really?" asked Frank. "That's pretty cool."

"I read about it in the paper," said Judy. "But where's Romeo?"

Judy looked in the water. Judy looked on top of the rocks. Romeo was nowhere to be found!

"Excuse me, students," a zookeeper said. "Unfortunately, Romeo the penguin is missing. We'll need you to leave the area while we search for him."

"Missing!" Judy exclaimed. "But everyone knows *both* penguin parents have to keep the egg warm and help it hatch! We need to find him!"

"Sorry, kids," said Mr. Todd, "Let's go check out Insecto Zone while the zoo-keepers look for Romeo."

"Insecto Zone? Gross, insects bug me,"

said Judy. *Plus, I absolutely, positively have to help find Romeo,* she thought.

Judy ducked behind a bench and watched the rest of her class follow Mr. Todd away from the bird area.

Once Class 3T was gone, she came out from behind the bench. The zoo-keeper who had told the class the bad news about Romeo was searching the area outside the fence. Judy went over to her. "Excuse me, Mrs. Baumgarten," Judy said, reading her name tag out loud. "I'd like to help you find Romeo."

"And who are you?" Mrs. Baumgarten asked.

"Judy Moody, Girl Detective. And pen-guin fan," Judy said.

"Shouldn't you be with your class?" said Mrs. Baumgarten.

"I'll catch up with them, I promise. But when was the last time you saw Romeo?" Judy asked, whipping out a pocket notebook and Grouchy pencil stub. She, Judy Moody, was on the case.

"Before the zoo closed last night, around six forty-five."

"Uh-huh. What was he doing when you saw him?" asked Judy.

"Romeo was near the fence, nibbling on a piece of squid. Juliet was sitting with the egg."

"Interesting," said Judy. *Scribble, scribble.*

A woman in a wet suit walked by.

"Hello, Miss Flores," Mrs. Baumgarten said. "Any sign of Romeo yet?"

"'Fraid not," Miss Flores said.

"When did you last see Romeo?" Judy asked Miss Flores.

"Last night," she said. "I got their dinner from the food-prep building and fed them, like I do every night, at six."

"What food did you get them?" asked Judy.

"Their usual: a bucket of squid. But the bucket I normally use was missing. I grabbed a smaller one and filled it to the very top with squid."

"Uh-huh, uh-huh," said Judy.

"After I fed the penguins, I went home for the night. I'm sure I latched the gate behind me, so I don't know how Romeo could have gotten out. The fence is high, and—"

"Penguins can't fly," said Judy. Miss Flores nodded.

Miss Flores went back to searching the area for signs of Romeo. Judy went back to searching, too. She studied the ground alongside the fence, hoping to find any sort of clue. But all she found was a hair elastic, an ice-cream wrapper, and a puddle of water.

Bang! Judy crashed right into another zoo worker—Mr. Gallagher. (All good detectives read name tags.) His walkie-talkie flew into the air and landed on the ground. He adjusted his glasses as he picked it up. "Well excuse me, young lady," he said. "I apologize. I'm quite distracted by this missing member of our zoo."

"Me, too," said Judy. "And I want to help. When was the last time *you* saw Romeo?"

"I went home around seven," Mr. Gallagher said. "Right after I finished unloading and stacking a shipment of ice blocks in the penguin habitat. King penguins like it cold, you know."

"Check. Uh-huh. What else?" Judy asked.

"That's about it. I locked the penguin

gate on my way out. That's the last time I saw Mr. Romeo. He was eating his dinner. In fact, I almost slipped on some of the squid that had spilled outside of the fence. I don't know how Romeo could have gotten out! Poor little guy. That egg's in its seventh week, about to hatch, and Juliet really needs him. She's been chirping and singing for him all day."

"Call Mrs. Baumgarten on your walkie-talkie!" Judy said. "I think I just-might-maybe know where Romeo is!" ๏

Turn the page to solve the mystery!

***How did Romeo escape,
and where does Judy
think he can be found?***

Romeo escaped by climbing up the ice blocks that Mr. Humphreys had stacked against the fence. He wanted to get to some squid that had dropped out of Miss Flores' bucket on the other side of the fence. By morning, the ice had melted, leaving a puddle, so it seemed impossible that Romeo could have climbed out.

Judy figured out that, after climbing out of his habitat on the ice blocks, Romeo must have followed Miss Flores's trail of dropped squid all the way to the food-prep building, where, sure enough, Judy and the zookeeper found him!

Use Your Noggin:
Way-Puzzling, Head-Scratching Logic Puzzles

Sometimes a mystery may seem uber-tricky and impossible to solve. In that case, a good way to think about it may be to use logic: narrowing down the possibilities until the conclusion is clear. Can you solve the following logic puzzles?

PLAYING FAVORITES

Judy's four friends each have a different favorite zoo animal. Someone's favorite is the polar bear, another person's favorite is the flamingo, another's is the alligator, and someone else's is the leopard. Can you figure out which person likes which animal based on the clues on the following page?

Hint: Keep track of the information in a chart. Draw an X in the box when you know a situation is not possible. Draw a check mark in the box to indicate a correct answer. For example, in this puzzle, you can draw an X in Frank's row for the animals that have fur, since you know from the clues that his favorite animal is fur-less. Check for the answers on page 123.

- Frank's favorite animal does not have fur.

- Jessica and Amy both like animals that have fur.

- Rocky likes an animal that has a long tail.

- Amy likes an animal that has spots.

CHEW ON THIS

Judy, Stink, Mom, and Dad get gumballs out of a bubble-gum machine. Four different flavors of gum come out: Ripe-Red Strawberry, Refreshing Minty Mint, Sour-Red Cherry, and Yellow Lemon. Can you use logic to figure out who got which flavor? Check for the answers on page 123.

- Judy got a red gumball.
- Stink got a gumball flavored like fruit.
- Neither Mom nor Dad got a red gumball.
- Mom got a non-fruit flavor.
- Judy did not get a cherry gumball.

Strawberry Mint Cherry Lemon

Judy

Stink

Mom

Dad

Mystery at Fur & Fangs

MINI-MYSTERY #2

Judy couldn't wait to teach her cat, Mouse, a new trick. Mouse already knew how to make toast. Now Judy was going to teach her how to turn off a light switch. But she needed some cat treats to do it.

"Mom! Dad! I'm going to Fur and Fangs!" Judy yelled. She strapped on her helmet and hopped on her bicycle. It was an extra-windy day. As Judy pedaled past the Speedy Market, she noticed that the wind had blown the P off of the sign. It now read S EEDY MARKET. Judy laughed.

Then she pedaled like lightning to the pet store, wind whipping through her hair.

At Fur and Fangs, Judy locked up her bike outside and went in. The wind blew the door shut behind her. Before she could ask Mrs. Birdwistle where the cat treats were, the pet-shop owner rushed over to Judy. "I just can't find it anywhere!" Mrs. Birdwistle said. She wiped her forehead and kept rummaging around the store, looking in boxes and under cages.

"Can't find what?" Judy asked. She was always in a girl-detective, solve-a-mystery mood.

"The shipment of guinea-pig food," Mrs. Birdwistle said. "It was supposed to have been delivered right here to six

Hummingbird Avenue
this morning. But now
it doesn't seem to be anywhere. Oh, my
poor little piggies. They must be getting
hungry." Judy heard a gaggle of guinea-
pig squeals from the cages in the corner.

"When was the last time you saw the
food?" asked Judy.

"I didn't actually see the shipment
come in," said Mrs. Birdwistle. "I've been
cleaning and feeding animals all morning. But it comes every Saturday morning
at this time."

Judy made a note in her detective notebook. Then she stepped outside to look
around the store entrance for clues.

Judy spotted the mail truck parked

across the street. Jack Frost! She ran over to say hi and ask him a question. But Jack Frost was not in his truck.

Judy saw the postman walking down the sidewalk, making deliveries. But the postman was not Jack Frost. "Excuse me," she called to him. "Isn't this Jack Frost's route?"

"Sure is. Except for some Saturdays. I'm the substitute postman. Name's Sam. Saturday Sam, they call me."

"Hi, Saturday Sam. I'm Judy. We're looking for a missing shipment of guinea-pig food. Did you make a delivery to Fur and Fangs by any chance?"

"That does ring a bell," said Sam. "I don't know if it was guinea-pig food, but I did have a cardboard box for six Hummingbird Ave. Yes, that's right—I delivered it earlier this morning!"

Judy wrote down *Saturday Sam— shipment to #6* in her notebook.

She, Judy Moody, had a for-real mystery on her hands. Fact #1: The box was not at Fur & Fangs. Fact #2: Postman Sam was sure he had delivered it.

Weird! This called for some serious sleuthing around the neighborhood. As in evidence. Judy looked up and down the street. All of the stores on the street had the same brass numbers nailed on their front doors.

First stop, Lots of Savings Bank next door at eight Hummingbird Avenue.

Maybe someone at the bank knew something about the food. Plus, the bank always had a bowl of lollipops on the counter, so it was worth a try. Her hair was blowing every which way in the wind. Judy tried to tamp it down as she stepped inside the bank.

Judy rushed up to the bank-teller's counter and said in her best detective voice, "Excuse me. If you were going to steal guinea-pig food, where would you put it?"

The bank teller answered, "I don't have a guinea pig, so I certainly wouldn't steal guinea-pig food. . . ."

"But if you did have a guinea pig, where would you put its food?"

"The best spot would be the bank safe, I suppose," said the teller.

"I'll need to take a look in the safe," said Judy.

"Sorry," said the teller, "Employees only. Nobody else is allowed in there."

Suspicious, thought Judy. She grabbed a free lollipop with a joke on the stick on her way out the door.

Next stop, nine Hummingbird Avenue. Roscoe's Flower Shop, across the street from Fur & Fangs.

The wind had knocked over a pot of geraniums and an umbrella stand on the front stoop. Roscoe was outside, hammering the brass number to the door.

"Go on inside out of the wind," he said. He opened the door and followed her inside.

Judy could barely see the floor. There were cardboard boxes, flowers, stems, and vases everywhere. "Well, hello!" said Roscoe. "Please don't mind the mess. I'm at sixes and nines with this wind today. It keeps knocking everything over and I have to haul it all inside."

"It's not the mess I'm worried about," said Judy. "It's the hungry guinea pigs."

"Hungry guinea pigs?" asked Roscoe.

"That's right," said Judy. "There's some piggy food missing from Fur and Fangs. Any idea where it might be?"

Roscoe waded through the vases and

flowers and boxes and over to Judy. He thought for a second. "Can't say that I know. Sorry kiddo. Gotta get back to fixing this mess."

ROAR! Judy stepped back outside. The wind flipped the pages of her notebook. Her head down, Judy hurried back toward Fur & Fangs.

Those poor piggies, she thought when she came to the front door of the pet store. She was about to open the door when she stopped. She stared at the brass number 6 nailed to the front of the store. She reread her notes. That's when it hit her.

"Mrs. Birdwistle, Mrs. Birdwistle! I know where the guinea-pig food is!" ☙

Turn the page to solve the mystery!

Where does Judy suspect the guinea-pig food is?

Judy realizes that the box of food must be among the mess at Roscoe's Flower Shop. When she arrived at the flower shop, Roscoe had been fixing the brass number on his front door. The wind must have caused the number on the shop to flip upside down, changing the number nine into a number six, the same address as Fur & Fangs. The food was not stolen—it was delivered by the substitute postman to the wrong address. Among the boxes and mess, Roscoe didn't realize that the box was in his store!

How to Draw a Suspect Sketch

But I can't draw! you might think. Don't worry; this is easy-peasier than you think! Once you boil things down, you'll be amazed at how many facts you can capture on paper.

HOW TALL WAS THE SUSPECT?

If you're not sure, try this:

- ◎ Picture the person standing against a door.

- ◎ Think about how high his or her head would be.

- ◎ Draw a mark (in pencil!) on a doorway at the height you think your suspect was.

- ◎ Measure the height of the mark. (The Women of Science Ruler does not lie!)

Example:

Suspect was about the height of a doorknob.

HOW OLD WAS THE SUSPECT?

If you're not good at guessing ages, consider these questions:

- Is anyone you know about the same size as the suspect?

- Did the suspect still have his baby teeth? If so, he's probably under the age of eight.

- Was the suspect missing a front tooth, or were his adult teeth growing in? If so, he's probably between the ages of eight and ten.

- Did the suspect have pimples on his face? If yes, he's probably older than fourteen.

- Did the suspect have a beard or mustache? He's probably older than seventeen.

Example:

> *No beard or mustache; a boy around 7–9 years old*

What other things about the person's mouth can the witness remember?

- Straight or crooked teeth?
- Braces or retainer?

- Sparkling white or discolored teeth?
- A small or wide mouth?

Example:

> *Straight white teeth;*
> *average-size mouth*

WHAT DID THE SUSPECT'S HAIR LOOK LIKE?

- Did the suspect have some white or gray hair? Chances are good he or she is a grown-up over the age of thirty.

- Did the suspect have a full head of white or gray hair? He or she is probably over the age of fifty.

- Was the person bald or balding?

- Was the person's hair dyed?

- Was the person's hair straight, wavy, or curly?

straight hair

wavy hair

curly hair

- Did the person wear his or her hair in a ponytail? Did he or she have bangs?

- Was his or her hair parted?

Example: *very spiky, blond hair; spikes make suspect appear taller than he really is.*

WHAT WAS THE SUSPECT'S SKIN COLOR?

Rather than just "white," "black," or "brown," try comparing the suspect's skin color to something concrete.

- Did it remind you of coffee with cream, honey, the skin of a peach?

- Did he or she have freckles?

- Were there any noticeable marks on the skin: tattoos, birthmarks, scars, moles?

Example: *skin the color of vanilla ice cream*

WHAT DID THE SUSPECT'S EYES LOOK LIKE?

- ◎ What color were the eyes?

- ◎ Was the person wearing glasses? Were the frames wire or plastic? What color? Were the lenses clear or tinted?

- ◎ Was the suspect wearing an eye patch?

Example:

blue eyes; no glasses

WHAT ABOUT THE SUSPECT'S CLOTHING?

Pants:

- ◎ Shorts or long pants?

- ◎ Denim or some other material?

- ◎ Belt? Unusually large or shaped buckle?

48

Shirt:

- ◉ Long-sleeved, short-sleeved, or tank top?
- ◉ Button-down, polo, or T-shirt?
- ◉ One or more colors?
- ◉ Any writing or design on the shirt?

Shoes:

- ◉ Sneakers or dress shoes? Laces or Velcro?

Accessories:

- ◉ Was the suspect wearing a hat, watch, jewelry, or any other accessory that you remember?

Example:

Suspect wore shorts (looked a little too long for him) and a plain blue T-shirt. He had dirty sneakers with a strong odor to them and wore a backpack.

The more you remember and the more you note, the more likely you are to narrow down your suspects.

Even if you find someone who *seems* a perfect match, assume that person is innocent! Time to start asking questions and making notes in your notebook.

Hint: *Start by questioning Stink!*

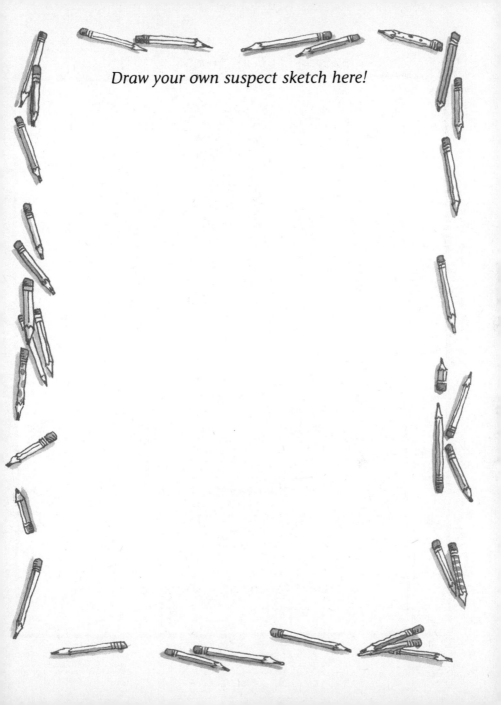

Draw your own suspect sketch here!

The Great Class 3T Pencil Heist

MINI-MYSTERY #3

Spelling test day! "Class 3T, please take out your pencils," said Mr. Todd. He passed around sheets of paper.

Jessica Finch was first to take out her pencil, of course. She was ready to get a 100 percent on the test. Or even 110 percent if there were bonus points! Frank took his pencil out of his pocket. Judy rustled through piles of papers and folders and notebooks. At last, she spotted her pencil on the floor. "Ready," Judy said to nobody.

"The first spelling word today is *detective*," said Mr. Todd.

Detective! Judy knew that word. For sure and absolute positive.

Rocky's hand shot up like a rocket. "Mr. Todd, I can't find my pencil anywhere. I think somebody stole it!"

The kids in Class 3T looked at one another with squinty eyes. A real-life pencil heist!

"I'm sure you just forgot where you put it," said Mr. Todd.

"But it's the one pencil that I've been using all year," said Rocky. "I wanted to use the same pencil every single day.

I was going to break the Virginia Dare School record! And now it's gone. I think somebody wanted my famous pencil."

"Who would want your pencil?" Frank asked.

"A pencil thief. That's who."

"Let's examine the facts," said Mr. Todd.

"Like detectives!" said Judy.

"What did your pencil look like?" asked Mr. Todd.

"It said JUST CANDY SWEET SHOP on it. It came from my all-time favorite candy shop."

"It must be around here somewhere," said Mr. Todd. "Pencils can't just get up and walk out of the classroom." Judy cracked up. Mr. Todd continued. "Frank, did you maybe pick up the wrong pencil by accident?"

"Nope," said Frank. "This is my I G♥ BASEBALL pencil. I got it at a baseball game last summer."

"I don't have it either," said Jessica. "The only pencil I have is Oinkerina." She held up a pinker-than-pink pencil with pictures of pigs doing ballet on it. "When you twirl it, the piggy ballerina eraser looks like she's dancing. See?"

"That's quite pig-tacular," said Mr. Todd.

"What about Judy?" asked Frank. "Maybe she has Rocky's pencil."

Judy made a face at Frank. "No chance, Lance!" she said. "I thought I lost my pencil, but I found it on the floor. It's a Name Your Pencil pencil. I sent away special to a catalog for a twelve pack. They all say JUDY'S on them. I've already used up four!"

"Amy, how about the pencil you're holding?" asked Mr. Todd.

"It's my new cupcake pencil. When you scratch-and-sniff it, it smells like cupcakes. Why would I want Rocky's super-stubby old pencil?"

"Hmm," thought Mr. Todd. "Class, how many days of school have we had so far?"

Judy looked at the countdown calendar on the wall. "Ninety-three!" she called out.

"That's right," said Mr. Todd. "So Rocky's pencil has gotten a lot of use. Rocky, how many times a day would you say you sharpen your pencil?"

"Um, at least three," Rocky said. "Sometimes more when it's a spelling test day or you give us extra word problems."

"I think I may know who our pencil thief is," said Mr. Todd, "but they didn't steal it." ☉

Turn the page to solve the mystery!

Who does Mr. Todd suspect has Rocky's pencil? And how did Mr. Todd know?

Mr. Todd knew that Rocky's pencil had the name of the Just Candy Sweet Shop on it, and that it had been sharpened many times. He also knew that the pencil was old and that some of the letters could have easily rubbed off.

Rocky's JUST CANDY SWEET SHOP pencil had been changed to:

Judy saw the pencil on the ground and accidentally picked it up, thinking it was hers.

Super-Sneaky Codes

Sometimes Judy Drewdy needs to pass along secret messages to Agent Dills Pickle, Agent Spuds Houdini, or even Agent James Madagascar. How do you get past super snoops and prying eyes? Secret codes, of course! Try cracking some of the top-secret codes below. Then try making up some of your own!

COLOR CODE

In this code, the only words that matter are the ones that come directly AFTER a color. Of course, only you and your friend know that, so the note will look like gibberish if anyone else sees it.

Can you decipher this note from Judy to Rocky and Frank?

Jaws Mr. Todd purple meet Virginia
yellow at pencil Band-Aid white the
spelling brown Toad Mouse backpack
green Pee Stink red Tent Nancy
Drew orange at detective black noon
magnifying glass.

ZIGZAG CODE

To decipher a zigzag code, read the letters in the first column from top to bottom, then go to the next column and read from top to bottom. Try deciphering these coded messages from Judy to Stink.

```
M M T Y U L S J W R A E
O A E O R A T A B E K R
```

```
Y U S E K R S I K
  O R N A E S T N
```

TELEPHONE CODE

To understand this code, look at how the letters are arranged on a telephone:

First, cross out the Q and the Z. Then, use the numbers on the phone buttons to indicate the letters you want to use. Since there are three letters for each number, indicate which of the three letters by using a "-" for the number on the left, a "0" for the number in the middle, and a "+" for the number on the right. So, the letter A would be written as 2-.

If you wanted to write "Hello" to a friend, you'd write:

40 30 5+ 5+ 6+

Can you decode this message from Judy to Mom and Dad?

2+ 2- 60 / 4+ / 7- 5+ 30 2- 7+ 30 /
40 2- 8+ 30 / 6- 6+ 70 30/
2- 5+ 5+ 6+ 9- 2- 60 2+ 30 /
8- 40 2- 60 / 7+ 8- 4+ 60 50?

P.S. Don't let your little "bother" get his mitts on your secret codebook!

BOOK CODE

Use the words in a favorite book to send messages to a friend! For each word in a book code, you'll see three numbers. The first number indicates the number of the page on which the word appears. The second number tells you the number of the line in which the word appears. And the third number tells you the word's position in the line, counting from left to right.

For example, let's say you want to tell your friend where a secret note is hidden. Using *Around the World in 8 1/2 Days,* your friend will find the note hidden in the:

119   2   3

Can you decipher the following code using this book as a guide?

26 5 7 / 48 7 3 /
92 2 3 / 49 9 4 /
7 2 1 / 40 2 6 /
20 3 4 / 7 8 1.

The Faux Artifact

MINI-MYSTERY #4

Judy doodled on the cover of her Social Studies book. "Can anyone tell me what an artifact is?" Mr. Todd asked Class 3T.

"Is it like a fact . . . about art?" Judy asked.

"Not quite," said Mr. Todd.

"I know," said Jessica Finch. "It's an old thing, right Mr. Todd?"

"That's true, it is something old.

An artifact is an object that can tell us something about the past. It can be *very* old, like a tool used by cave dwellers. It can be something more recent too, like a letter your mother wrote, or even a toy you played with when you were a baby."

"So, Stink's baby belly button that he keeps in a jar is an artifact?" Judy asked.

"Yes, because it's an object that helps tell the story of Stink's past," said Mr. Todd. "Your homework tonight is to look around your house and find an artifact. Ask your parents for help. There may be old artifacts in your house you don't even know about. We'll share them with the class tomorrow."

☺   ☺   ☺

"I know what artifact I'm going to bring," Rocky said later at lunch. "My grandfather rode across Europe on a bicycle when he was a teenager. And he kept a diary about it."

"Cool," said Frank. "I'm going to bring a doll that belonged to my mom's aunt. It's over fifty years old!"

"My mom and dad have a spoon made by THE Paul Revere himself," said Judy. "I'm going to ask if I can bring that."

"Wow!" said Rocky and Frank. "That's waaay old."

Jessica Finch said, "I'm going to bring in an artifact older than any of yours. Way better than some old spoon."

❂   ❂   ❂

The next day, Class 3T gathered in a circle to share their artifacts. Rocky showed his grandfather's journal, Frank showed his great-aunt's doll, and Judy showed her Paul Revere spoon.

"My mom doesn't let me eat with this spoon, though," Judy said. "She says it's just for looking at since it's so old. Paul Revere made it at his silversmith shop in 1757."

"That's quite an old artifact," said Mr. Todd. "Thanks very much for sharing it with us. Jessica, would you like to show the class what you brought?"

"I'd love to. My artifact is way older than Judy's or anybody's. It's an invitation from the pilgrims to the Native

Americans inviting them to the very first Thanksgiving." Jessica held up a piece of wrinkly paper that was yellowed around the edges and had cursive writing on it. She read the letter aloud:

November 31, 1621

Dear Chief Massasoit,
    We the Pilgrims of Plimoth Colony invite ye and your men to our table for the first ever Thanksgiving dinner.

Signed,
Governor William Bradford

"Neato! A real letter from 1621!" Frank said.

"Awesome!" said Rocky. The class buzzed with chatter.

Judy raised her hand. "Yes, Judy?" asked Mr. Todd.

"That letter isn't older than my spoon," Judy said.

"Yes it is," said Jessica. "Way older— more than one hundred and thirty years older!"

"I don't think so," Judy said. "It's not even a real artifact. It's a big fat fake. And I can prove it."

Turn the page to solve the mystery!

How did Judy know that Jessica's letter was a fake?

The first clue that the letter was forged was the date. November only has thirty days, so there was no way the letter could have been written on November 31.

The other clue was that the letter mentions the "first Thanksgiving." At the time, the Pilgrims couldn't have known that the meal would become a tradition, and so they wouldn't have called it "first." In fact, Thanksgiving was not declared a national holiday until more than 200 years later in 1863 by President Lincoln.

Wink, Wink, Murder!

Holy macaroni! Is there a murderer among your friends? At your sleepover? At your birthday party? In the Toad Pee Club?

You be the detective! Sleuth out the murderer as quick as a wink in the game **Wink, Wink, Murder!**

Want to play? Here's how:

You'll need a group of five or six friends and a deck of cards. Form a circle. You will need as many cards as you have people. Make sure the cards contain the Ace of Spades (Murderer) and Queen of Hearts (Detective).

❀ Take turns being dealer. The dealer shuffles the cards and passes them out facedown.

❀ Look at your card secretly. Do not let anybody see who is the Murderer.

❀ The player who gets the Queen of Hearts holds it up for all to see. He or she is the Detective and will sit in the middle of the circle.

- The job of the Murderer is to bump off as many players as possible *without getting caught*. To do this, the murderer must wink at someone in the circle without being spotted by the detective.

- One by one, as players are bumped off, they must dramatically fall back and pretend to die.

- Give the detective at least three chances to catch the criminal.

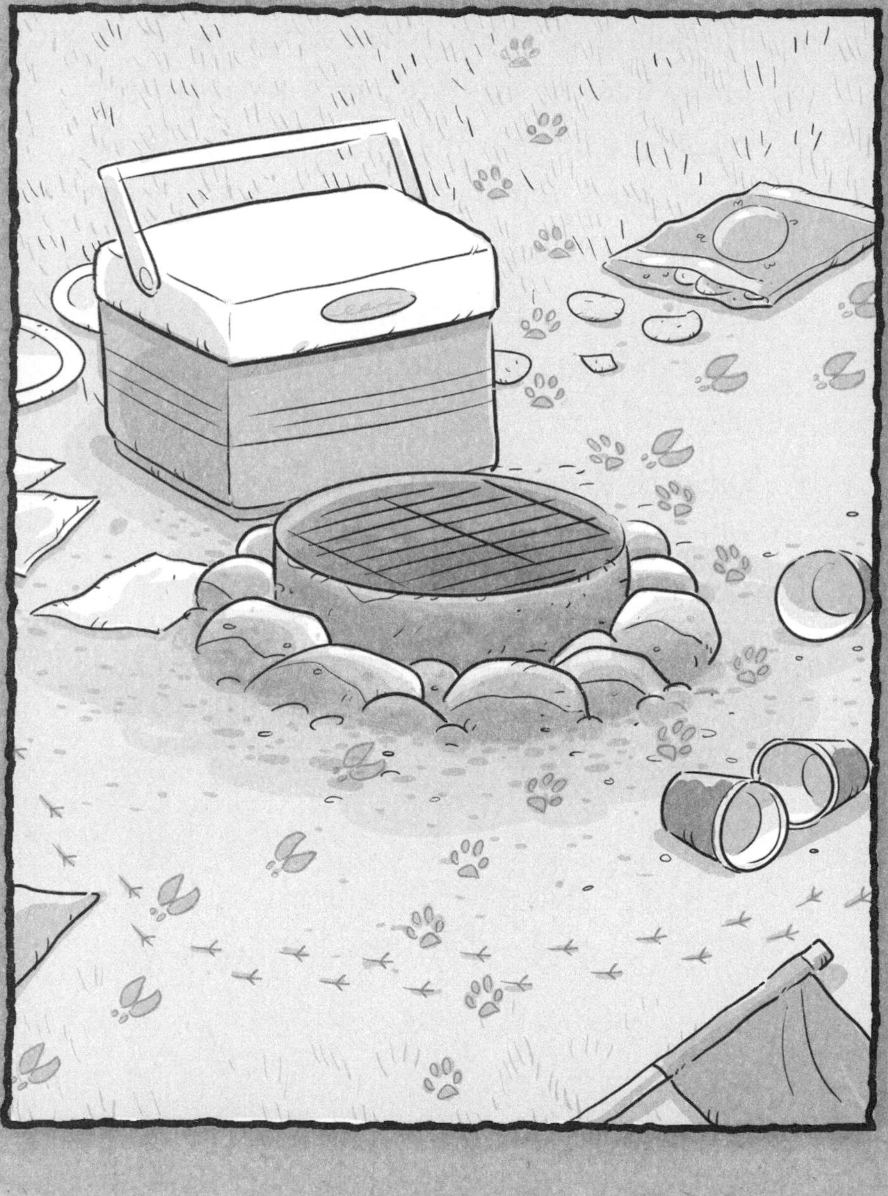

The Disappearing Hamburger

MINI-MYSTERY #5

Judy was in a back-to-nature mood. A get-muddy, cook-s'mores-over-a-fire, sleep-under-the-stars mood. The Moody family was going camping for the weekend. She, Judy Moody, was ready to be one with the wild.

The Moodys pitched a tent at their campsite. Stink pitched a fit about mosquitoes. Mom laid out food for lunch.

"Mmm, burgers!" Judy said.

"The meat has to defrost," Mom said. "Why don't we go for a nature walk?"

Judy, Stink, Mom, and Dad headed to the ranger station.

"Howdy! I'm Ranger Jill," said the ranger. "I'll be leading our walk in the woods. Are you ready to learn about some of the flora and fauna of the area?"

"Floor-y and yawn-a?" Judy let out a yawn.

"Flora and fauna," said Ranger Jill. "It means plants and animals."

Animals! Judy perked up.

"Before we go into the woods, here are nature notebooks for everyone. They describe some of the animals that make these woods their home. There's space in the back for you to record your own sightings."

"Rare!" said Judy. She opened the notebook. Photos of a fox, a deer, and a woodpecker stared back at her.

Ranger Jill led the campers down a trail. "In the back of your notebooks, you'll find a chart of common animal tracks. See if you can find some of them on our walk. Tracks can tell you a lot about an animal: how fast they were going, whether they were with other animals, and where they were headed."

Fox

Deer

Bird

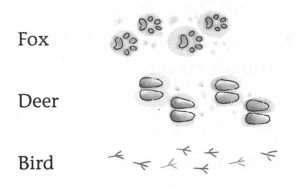

Judy looked at the chart. She looked down at the ground. She saw lots and lots of flora. But not one single fauna. And no fauna tracks.

The group kept walking. Judy spotted a not-flying squirrel (bor-ing) and an ant (double-boring).

"Look for snapped-off twigs," said Ranger Jill. "And you might find deer hoofprints. Deer eat only plants. They like to nibble on leaves and twigs."

Snap! Snap! The only snapped-off twigs Judy saw were the ones made by Stink.

"What if we see a dead skunk?" asked Stink. "Does that mean a bear was here?"

"Maybe," said Ranger Jill. "Bears do eat some small mammals."

"If we see a dead skunk, the only tracks will be mine," said Judy, holding her nose. "Running away."

Before long, they were back to the ranger station. "I didn't even see one animal track on our nature walk," said Judy.

"Well, I saw a newt," said Stink. "And an endangered Virginia round-leaf birch tree."

Back at the campsite, Dad cut up some watermelon and Mom poured lemonade. "Judy, could you bring me the hamburger meat, please?" Mom said. "I left it on a tree stump near the fire pit."

"It's not there!" said Judy. "Unless we're having invisible burgers."

"Well that's a mystery," said Mom. "I

could have sworn I left the meat right there."

"Cool, burgers that evaporate!" said Stink. "Poof!"

"I must have just misplaced it," said Mom. She and Dad began searching through the cooler and grocery bags.

Judy went to the stump where Mom had left the meat and crouched down. There were faint markings in the dirt around the stump. "Fauna footprints!" Judy said. "As in for-real animal tracks. No lie." She took her nature notebook out of her pocket and drew a sketch of what she saw.

"Mom, you didn't misplace the meat.

And it didn't evaporate. A hungry critter from nature took it!"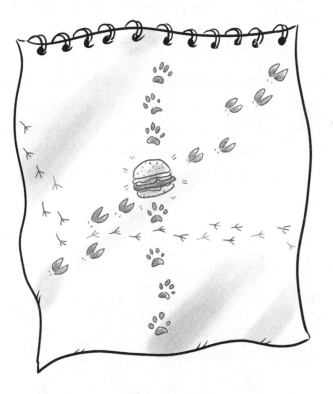

Turn the page to solve the mystery!

Which animal does Judy suspect ate the hamburger meat?

Based on the animal tracks, Judy thinks that a fox stole the food. The bird tracks do not go close enough to the food for the bird to have eaten it. The deer tracks do go near the food, but deer do not eat meat, so the fox is the likely culprit.

Hair-Pulling Head-Scratchers

◉ Frank Pearl (aka Dills Pickle) had a pickle of a puzzle for Judy. What eight-letter word contains only ONE letter?

It took Judy two Grouchy pencils and three erasers to figure this one out. Can you solve it?

◉ Presto Whammo! Rocky (aka Spuds Houdini) produced a pickle puzzle of his own. What's another eight-letter word that contains only one letter?

◉ Judy and Stink stepped on the same piece of paper at the same time.

"Mine!" said Judy.

"Mine!" said Stink. Though Judy and Stink stood face-to-face on the same piece of paper, it was impossible for them to touch each other. How could this be?

Answers on page 123

Test Your Powers of Observation

One of the most important skills of a detective is noticing what's going on around her. Look at the picture on page 91 for ten seconds, and then try answering the questions without looking back.

Turn the page to see how many facts you can remember from this picture!

Easy:

1. What animal is licking Judy?

2. How many people are in the picture?

Medium:

3. Who is walking into the tent?

4. Who is laying on the ground?

5. What is on Frank's face?

Difficult:

6. How many cookies are on the ground?

Turn to page 124 to see how much you remembered!

*Turn the page to see how many facts you
can remember from this picture!*

Easy:

1. How many people are in the picture?

Medium:

2. What is in Judy's bag?

3. What is behind Judy's ear?

4. What is on Stink's T-shirt?

Difficult:

5. How many watches is Judy wearing?

6. What is around Dad's neck?

7. What is on Judy's thumb?

Turn to page 124 to see how much you remembered!

Be a Nancy Drew Gumshoe
A Nancy Drew Mystery

Calling all super-sleuths! When Judy made her list of Nancy Drew books, Stink was bugging her and she made thirteen mistakes. Can you find all thirteen of the Moody mix-ups in the list? Go to the library or search online if you need help.

#1:   *The Secret of the Old Clock* (1930)

#2:   *The Hidden Staircase* (1930)

#3:   *The Bungalow Mystery* (1930)

#4:   *The Mystery at Lilac Inn* (1930)

#5:   *The Secret at Shadow Ranch* (1931)

#6:   *The Secret of Pink Gate Farm* (1931)

#7:   *The Clue in the Diary* (1932)

#8:   *Nancy's Mysterious Letter* (1932)

#9:   *The Sign of the Twisted Candles* (1933)

#10: *The Password to Larkspur Lane* (1933)

#11: *The Clue of the Broken Locket* (1934)

#12: *The Message in the Hollow Oak* (1935)

#13: *The Mystery of the Ivory Bad Luck Charm* (1936)

#14: *The Screaming Mimi Statue* (1937)

#15: *The Haunted Bridge* (1937)

#16: *The Clue of the Tapping Heels* (1939)

#17: *The Mystery of the Brass-Bound Trunk* (1940)

#18: *The Mystery at the Moss-Covered Mansion* (1941)

#19: *The Quest of the Missing Map* (1942)

#20: *The Clue in the Grouchy Pencil Box* (1943)

#21: *The Secret in the Old Attic* (1944)

#22: *The Clue in the Crumbling Wall* (1945)

#23: *The Mystery of the Liberty Bell* (1946)

#24: *The Clue in the Old Album* (1947)

#25: *The Ghost of Blackwood Hall* (1948)

#26: *The Clue of the Leaning Chimney* 1949)

#27: *The Secret of the Wooden Leg* (1950)

#28: *The Clue of the Black Keys* (1951)

#29: *The Mystery at the Ski Jump* (1952)

#30: *The Clue of the Velvet Mask* (1953)

#31: *The Ringmaster's Secret* (1953)

#32: *The Scarlet Slipper Mystery* (1954)

#33: *The Witch Tree Symbol* (1955)

#34: *The Hidden Window Mystery* (1956)

#35: *The Haunted Root-Beer Float* (1957)

#36: *The Secret of the Golden Palamino* (1959)

#37: *The Clue in the Old Stagecoach* (1960)

#38: *The Mystery of the Fire Dragon* (1961)

#39: *The Clue of the Roaring Puppet* (1962)

#40: *The Moonstone Castle Mystery* (1963)

#41: *The Clue of the Whistling Bagpipes* (1964)

#42: *The Phantom of Pine Hill* (1965)

#43: *The Mystery of the 99 Steps* (1966)

#44: *The Clue in the Crossword Cipher* (1967)

#45: *The Eight-and-a-Half-Legged Spider Sapphire Mystery* (1968)

#46: *The Invisible Intruder* (1969)

#47: *The Mysterious Mouse* (1970)

#48: *The Crooked Banister* (1971)

#49: *The Secret of Mirror Bay* (1972)

#50: *The Double-Rare Jinx Mystery* (1973)

#51: *Mystery of the Glowing Eye* (1974)

#52: *The Secret of the Forgotten City* (1975)

#53: *The Sky Phantom* (1976)

#54: *The Strange Message in the Parchment* (1977)

#55: *Mystery of Artichoke Island* (1978)

#56: *The Thirteenth Pearl* (1979)

Judy Moody can't wait to read and collect all the classic Nancy Drew Mysteries. How many of these titles can you find in *Judy Moody, Girl Detective?* You be the Judy Drewdy! Answers can be found on pages 124–125.

Want more Nancy Drew?
Read the following short story.

Judy Moody and the Mystery of the Missing Mood Ring

Judy Moody was walking with her nose in Nancy Drew #32, *The Scarlet Slipper Mystery*, when—*BAM!*—she ran smack-dab into a fourth-grader. A fourth-grader carrying a giant stack of library books. The books went flying. OOPS!

"Sorry!" Judy and the girl said at the same time.

Judy helped pick up the books. "*Secret in the Old Attic?*" she said. "*The Hidden Staircase?*"

"I'm freaky for Nancy Drew," said the girl.

"I'm freaky for Nancy Drew! I'm reading all fifty-six classic Nancy Drews. I'm on number thirty-two."

"Hey, don't I know you? We played soccer together last summer. I go to Jerabek Elementary School, but my mom knows your mom. My name's Alyssa."

"Oh, yeah!" said Judy.

Before you could say "Scarlet Slipper," Judy had a playdate with Alyssa.

❧   ❧   ❧

Judy's mom pulled up outside Alyssa's house. It had purple front steps, a porch covered in vines, and a round tower.

"This looks like a haunted house!" said Stink. "No way would I go in there."

The house did look way old and spooky.

Judy glanced at her mood ring. Amber. Amber was for *Nervous*. Amber was for *Not-So-Sure*. Amber seemed to whisper, *Never-Go-Inside-Haunted-Houses.*

Judy reached into the pocket where she kept her SOS lipstick. It helped her pluck up her courage. She climbed the purple steps and knocked on the front door.

Alyssa opened the door, and Judy stepped inside. The first thing Judy noticed was a chandelier in the entryway—it was swinging back and forth. Then, from out of nowhere, spooky music drifted into the room.

Judy got goose bumps, *goose eggs.*

Alyssa didn't seem to notice a thing.

"Is this house haunted?" Judy whispered.

"Of course not." Alyssa laughed. "Don't be cuckoo." Judy started to relax. Alyssa lowered her voice. "Sometimes I *do* hear spooky sounds coming from the attic. You want to go up?"

"Up? As in stairs? To the spooky attic?" Judy checked her mood ring. *Blue-green?* Blue-green was for *Relaxed, Calm.* She, Judy Moody, did not feel *Relaxed, Calm* at all!

Upstairs, Alyssa yanked a rope in the ceiling. Down came a secret staircase that led into the attic. Jeepers! The cobwebby attic was full of junk covered in million-year-old dust: chairs, rolls of carpet, old-timey paintings, a cracked mirror.

Just then, out of the corner of Judy's eye, something caught her attention. Something in the mirror. Something hairy and scary.

"AGHHHHHH!" Judy screamed and fell back on the floor. She scrambled back up to her feet and made a beeline for the stairs. "I think . . . saw . . . gorilla . . . ghost!"

"Judy! Stop! Wait!"

But Judy didn't stop. She didn't wait. Judy flew down the attic stairs, through the front door, and out into the sunshine as fast as she could, all the way home.

❧   ❧   ❧

Judy tried not to think about haunted houses. She tried not to think about swinging chandeliers and spooky music. She tried not to think about gorillas or ghosts.

She, Judy Moody, was in a mood. A tingle-up-your-spine mood. *What color is my mood ring?* She looked down at her hand.

Hello! Her mood ring! It was G-O-N-E, gone! This was a for-real mystery for Judy Moody, Girl Detective: *Mystery of the Missing Mood Ring.*

When had she last seen it? At breakfast. At soccer. In the car with Stink . . .

Stink!

Judy Drewdy went to find her number-one suspect. She shone a flashlight in Stink's eyes. "Where's my mood ring?" she asked a million and one times. Judy held up an apple but wouldn't let him eat it. Yet.

"Honest to pizza! I did NOT steal it! You had it on in the car. I saw you checking it. Maybe that gorilla ATE your mood ring."

The gorilla! Of course! She'd had her mood ring on in the attic just before . . . .

Wait just a Nancy Drew minute! This was exactly like . . . Nancy Drew Book #2, *The Hidden Staircase*. Nancy goes to a creepy mansion, sees the creepy chandelier swinging, hears creepy music, finds a creepy hidden staircase, and sees a creepy gorilla at the window.

Maybe Alyssa's house was haunted after all! And, she, Judy Moody, had to go back there to get her ring. *Brrr.* Judy shivered at the thought.

ଶ   ଶ   ଶ

Alyssa opened the front door. She looked surprised to see Judy.

"Hey, have you seen my mood ring?" Judy asked Alyssa.

"Mood ring?" Alyssa said. "You had it on when we went upstairs."

"Then I think your house is haunted for *real,*" Judy said.

Alyssa howled like a hyena. "I got you! I got you so good!"

"You mean—all that spooky stuff was just a big fat fake-out?"

"I got the idea to spook you from reading *The Hidden Staircase*. So I asked my brother to jump on his bed to make the chandelier swing, play creepy music, and hide up in the attic with his gorilla mask. Judy Moody, you cracked the case!"

"RARE!" said Judy. "But—there's still the Mystery of the Missing Mood Ring."

❧　❧　❧

Judy and Alyssa crawled on hands and knees across the attic floor, searching for her mood ring. "I'm sure you just dropped it," said Alyssa. *But where was it?*

"I guess my mood ring is *not in the mood* to be found," said Judy. All of a sudden, her hand pressed down on a loose floorboard. The board popped up. Under the loose board was . . . a way-cool secret compartment!

"My ring!" shouted Judy, sliding it onto her finger. "I guess it flew off yesterday when I saw your brother the gorilla, and it fell though a crack."

Alyssa peered into the dark hole. "Hey, what's this?" She picked something up and blew on it. A cloud of dust cleared. A note! The note was in a secret code.

OLLP RM GSV IZUGVIH.
Signed,
Nancy Drew's biggest fan,
Alice Sutherland

December 29, 1930

"Alice in Wonderland left us a secret code from 1930?" Judy screeched.

"No, silly. *Alice Sutherland.* She must have lived in this house a way long time ago! She read Nancy Drew, too. How cool is that? Just think: she left this note for us to find someday. It's like an eighty-year-old mystery."

"That's older than my grandma Lou!"

Judy stared at the secret code. "It's a classic reverse alphabet code. You know, where the letter *A* equals *Z*?" The girls got a pencil and worked out the code.

LOOK IN THE RAFTERS.

Judy and Alyssa searched the attic up and down. "I think I see something blue back here!" Alyssa shouted, reaching up into the rafters. She pulled down a musty, dusty old book. "Nancy Drew book number two. *The Hidden Staircase!* It's like the one I got from the library, only way old."

Holy macaroni! Judy barely dared to breathe.

"I bet this is one of the first Nancy Drew books ever. It must be worth a bazillion dollars!" Alyssa cracked open the book. "Look! She wrote something in fancy handwriting."

Judy peered over Alyssa's shoulder, reading the inscription.

Dear Girl in the Future,
If you are holding this book, you
have solved my Mystery in the
Attic Rafters. You are just
like Nancy Drew!
A. S.

"Same-same!" said Judy, grinning at Alyssa. ⊚

Nancy Drew Facts

WHO IS CAROLYN KEENE?

Nancy Drew books are written by author Carolyn Keene, right? Wrong!

Carolyn Keene is a made-up name for several writers who penned Nancy Drew books. Two of the original writers of Nancy Drew books were Mildred Wirt Benson and Harriet Stratemeyer Adams.

Author Megan McDonald was very tricky when she wrote *Judy Moody, Girl Detective,* and she used those names for two of her characters. Can you find characters in *Judy Moody, Girl Detective* with the names Mildred Benson and Mrs. Stratemeyer?

WHO SAID IT?

Nancy Drew sure had some funny sayings and expressions. Look at the list of stuff Judy Moody says in *Judy Moody, Girl Detective* and try to figure out which ones came from Nancy Drew.

Hint: *Nancy Drew's sayings might sound old-fashioned.*

- ☻ Jeepers!
- ☻ Cool Beans!
- ☻ RARE!
- ☻ Crumbs!
- ☻ Scoo-bee-doo!
- ☻ Hankie
- ☻ Easy-peasy, lemon-squeezy

- ☻ Holy jeepers!
- ☻ Chums
- ☻ Hypers!
- ☻ Crumbs to that
- ☻ Chips ahoy!
- ☻ Penny loafers
- ☻ Vexed
- ☻ Flushie

FIND THE BAD GUYS

Nancy Drew has met some real bad guys in her time. Which of the following are real bad guys from a classic Nancy Drew book? And which are names that Stink made up?

◉ Stumpy	◉ Snuffy
◉ Stingy	◉ Snorky
◉ Scurvy	◉ Grumpy
◉ Grumper	◉ Sniggs
◉ Snarky	

NANCY DREW WISDOM

Judy Moody is a girl detective. You can be, too. Can you detect what this means? It's one of Judy's favorite sayings.

N.L.H.W.A.B.P.

(Never Leave Home
Without A Bobby Pin)

Why does Judy say this? Because Nancy Drew always carried a bobby pin and used it to pick locks and get out of other tricky situations!

FINGERPRINT PATTERNS

Collecting fingerprints is a snap! Use a paint-brush to lightly dust powder onto a surface where fingerprints are likely to be. The powder will stick to the oils left behind by a person's skin. Lay a piece of clear tape over the print, then slowly lift it back up and stick it to a piece of black paper to "collect" the print for your records. Use the pictures below to categorize any fingerprints you find. Then, when you're interviewing a suspect, compare the person's fingerprints to the ones at the scene of the crime.

loop

arch

whorl

COMMUNICATING WITH MORSE CODE

Morse code is a way of communicating using lights or sounds of different lengths. Girl detective Nancy Drew knew how to send messages in Morse code using the heels of her shoes to make clicking noises!

A	· —	N	— ·	1	· — — — —
B	— · · ·	O	— — —	2	· · — — —
C	— · — ·	P	· — — ·	3	· · · — —
D	— · ·	Q	— — · —	4	· · · · —
E	·	R	· — ·	5	· · · · ·
F	· · — ·	S	· · ·	6	— · · · ·
G	— — ·	T	—	7	— — · · ·
H	· · · ·	U	· · —	8	— — — · ·
I	· ·	V	· · · —	9	— — — — ·
J	· — — —	W	· — —	0	— — — — —
K	— · —	X	— · · —		
L	· — · ·	Y	— · — —		
M	— —	Z	— — · ·		

Try deciphering these messages in Morse code:

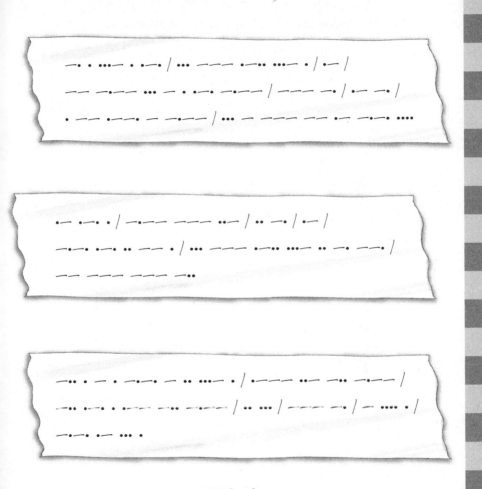

See page 126 for the answers.

HANDWRITING ANALYSIS

A good detective can learn a lot about a person from her handwriting. Use these helpful tips if you find handwritten evidence at a crime scene.

Slant:

slanting to right

Writer is open and likes to socialize.

slanting to left

Writer is shy and likes to be left alone.

no slant

Writer is logical and shows little emotion.

Size:

Writer has a big personality and likes attention.

large

Writer is focused and can concentrate easily.

small

Writer is calm.

average

Loops:

ℓ ← loop is tight

Writer is stressed or tense.

ℓ ← loop is loose

Writer is carefree and spontaneous.

# Rules for Being a Good Detective

- Never leave home without a bobby pin.

- Never solve a mystery on an empty stomach.

- Don't be afraid to ask for help.

- Always keep a sense of humor and an open mind.

- Do not get in a bad mood. It can cloud your judgment and cause you to over-look important details.

- Everyone's a suspect. (But don't forget, everyone is innocent until proven guilty!)

- Never give up.

- A detective's work is never done.

Answer Key

USE YOUR NOGGIN: WAY-PUZZLING, HEAD-SCRATCHING LOGIC PUZZLES

1. Frank = flamingo;
   Jessica = polar bear;
   Amy = leopard;
   Rocky = alligator

2. Judy = strawberry;
   Stink = cherry;
   Mom = mint;
   Dad = lemon

SUPER-SNEAKY CODES

Color Code:
Meet at the Toad Pee Tent at noon

Zigzag Code:
1. Mom ate your last jawbreaker

2. Your sneakers stink

Telephone Code:
Can I please have more allowance than Stink?

BOOK CODE

1. Encyclopedia

2. The suspect is wearing sunglasses and a hat.

HAIR-PULLING HEAD-SCRATCHERS:

1. ENVELOPE (one letter was inside the envelope)

2. TOLERATE (the word LETTER is scrambled in the word TOLERATE)

3. Judy and Stink are standing on opposite sides of a solid door. The piece of paper is on the floor under the door.

TEST YOUR POWERS OF OBSERVATION

Picure #1
1. dog
2. four
3. Stink
4. Judy, Rocky, and Frank
5. glasses
6. five

Picture #2
1. three
2. notebook and pencil
3. pencil
4. a picture of Stink
5. two
6. scarf
7. mood ring

How many questions did you get right?

1–4: Nice try! Keep practicing your observation skills.

5–8: You're a good detective! With a little more practice, you'll be as good as Judy Drewdy.

9–13: You're an eagle-eyed super-sleuth! There's no mystery you can't solve.

BE A NANCY DREW GUMSHOE

Judy made 13 mistakes in her list of Nancy Drew books. Here are the real titles.

#6 *The Secret of Red Gate Farm*
#13 *The Mystery of the Ivory Charm*
#14 *The Whispering Statue*
#20 *The Clue in the Jewel Box*
#23 *The Mystery of the Tolling Bell*
#27 *The Secret of the Wooden Lady*
#35 *The Haunted Showboat*
#36 *The Secret of the Golden Pavilion*
#39 *The Clue of the Dancing Puppet*
#45 *The Spider Sapphire Mystery*
#47 *The Mysterious Mannequin*
#50 *The Double Jinx Mystery*
#55 *Mystery of Crocodile Island*

14 different titles are mentioned in *Judy Moody, Girl Detective* (a few are mentioned more than once).

p. 4: *Message in the Hollow Oak*
p. 7: *Mystery of the 99 Steps*
p. 14 *Phantom of Pine Hill*
p. 54 *The Haunted Bridge*
pp. 66, 145 *The Password to Larkspur Lane*
p. 75 *The Witch Tree Symbol*
p. 86 *The Sign of the Twisted Candles*
pp. 93, 137, 168 *The Secret of the Old Clock*

p. 94 *The Mystery of the Brass Bound Trunk*
p. 94 *The Mystery at Lilac Inn*
p. 94 *The Ghost of Blackwood Hall*
p. 107 *The Secret of Shadow Ranch*
p. 128 *The Clue in the Crumbling Wall*
p. 155 *The Mystery of the Moss-Covered Mansion*

WHO IS CAROLYN KEENE?:
p. 133 Mrs. Stratemeyer
p. 124 Mildred Benson

WHO SAID IT?:

Phrase	Page in *JM,GD*	Answer
Jeepers!	5	Nancy
Cool Beans!	151	Judy
RARE!	168	Judy
Crumbs!	29	Nancy
Scoo-bee-doo!	32	Judy
Hankie	37	Nancy

Easy-peasy, lemon-squeezy	161	Judy
Holy jeepers!	157	Judy
Chums	89	Nancy
Hypers!	128	Nancy
Crumbs to that	141	Nancy
Chips ahoy!	151	Judy
Penny loafers	168	Nancy
Vexed	142	Nancy
Flushie	103	Judy

FIND THE BAD GUYS:

Real bad guys are:

Stumpy	(p. 59)
Sniggs	(p. 59)
Snorky	(p. 59)
Grumper	(p. 14)

Stink's bad guys are:

Grumpy	(p. 71)
Scurvy	(p. 71)
Snarky	(p. 83)
Snuffy	(p. 83)
Stingy	(p. 83)

COMMUNICATING WITH MORSE CODE

1. Never solve a mystery on an empty stomach
2. Are you in a crime solving mood
3. Detective Judy Drewdy is on the case

Text copyright © 2012 by Megan McDonald
Judy Moody font copyright © 2003 by Peter H. Reynolds
Judy Moody®. Judy Moody is a registered trademark of Candlewick Press, Inc.
Nancy Drew is a registered trademark of Simon & Schuster, Inc.

"Judy Moody and the Mystery of the Missing Mood Ring"
copyright © 2010 by Megan McDonald

Illustrations from:
Judy Moody copyright © 2000 by Peter H. Reynolds
Judy Moody Gets Famous copyright © 2001 by Peter H. Reynolds
Judy Moody Saves the World! copyright © 2002 by Peter H. Reynolds
Judy Moody Predicts the Future copyright © 2003 by Peter H. Reynolds
Judy Moody, M.D.: The Doctor Is In! copyright © 2004 by Peter H. Reynolds
Judy Moody Declares Independence copyright © 2005 by Peter H. Reynolds
Judy Moody Around the World in 8½ Days copyright © 2006 by Peter H. Reynolds
Judy Moody Goes to College copyright © 2008 by Peter H. Reynolds
Judy Moody, Girl Detective copyright © 2010 by Peter H. Reynolds
Judy Moody and the NOT Bummer Summer copyright © 2012 by Peter H. Reynolds
Stink: The Incredible Shrinking Kid copyright © 2005 by Peter H. Reynolds
Stink-O-Pedia Volume Two copyright © 2010 by Peter H. Reynolds
Judy Moody's Way Wacky Uber Awesome Book of More Fun Stuff to Do
copyright © 2010 by Candlewick Press, created by Matt Smith
All other illustrations created by Matt Smith, copyright © 2012 by Candlewick Press

First edition 2012

Library of Congress Cataloging-in-Publication Data is available.
Library of Congress Catalog Card Number 2011048353
ISBN 978-0-7636-5941-7

13 14 15 16 17 BVG 10 9 8 7 6 5
Printed in Berryville, VA, U.S.A.

This book was typeset in Stone Informal and Judy Moody.
The illustrations were done in watercolor, tea, and ink, or were created digitally.

Candlewick Press
99 Dover Street
Somerville, Massachusetts 02144

visit us at www.candlewick.com